Samuel French Acting Edition

When Men Are Scarce

by John Kirkpatrick

SAMUELFRENCH.COM   SAMUELFRENCH.CO.UK

FOR PRODUCTION ENQUIRIES

UNITED STATES AND CANADA

Info@SamuelFrench.com
1-866-598-8449

UNITED KINGDOM AND EUROPE

Plays@SamuelFrench.co.uk
020-7255-4302

Each title is subject to availability from Samuel French, depending upon country of performance. Please be aware that *WHEN MEN ARE SCARCE* may not be licensed by Samuel French in your territory. Professional and amateur producers should contact the nearest Samuel French office or licensing partner to verify availability.

MUSIC USE NOTE

Licensees are solely responsible for obtaining formal written permission from copyright owners to use copyrighted music in the performance of this play and are strongly cautioned to do so. If no such permission is obtained by the licensee, then the licensee must use only original music that the licensee owns and controls. Licensees are solely responsible and liable for all music clearances and shall indemnify the copyright owners of the play(s) and their licensing agent, Samuel French, against any costs, expenses, losses and liabilities arising from the use of music by licensees. Please contact the appropriate music licensing authority in your territory for the rights to any incidental music.

IMPORTANT BILLING AND CREDIT REQUIREMENTS

If you have obtained performance rights to this title, please refer to your licensing agreement for important billing and credit requirements.

CHARACTERS

DIANE

OLIVE

MAUDIE

SUE

JUNE

MRS. EDWARDS

SCENE: An apartment in a walk-up in the East Eighties, New York City.

TIME: Late afternoon in November.

When Men are Scarce

SCENE: *The room is nicely furnished, warm-looking and attractive. The front door is at Right, opening on, with its hinges Upstage. Below it is a straight chair, and above it a long table on which are a lamp and two silver bowls, or bonbon dishes. Right Center, placed in a diagonal position, is a low-backed sofa. Before sofa is a coffee table on which are magazines and an ashtray. At Left is an archway to hall which leads to the rest of the apartment—bedrooms, kitchen, etc. Downstage from arch is a wing chair and Upstage a lowboy, or chest of drawers, with a lamp on top of it. Left Center is a gate-leg table, partially unfolded. There is a side chair above it and one on either side. In the Upstage wall, Right of Center, is a fairly large window, provided with drapes and a shade that is drawn down about half way. There are three or four potted plants on the wide sill. Outside the window is an iron fire escape, with a railing, and steps going up from Left to Right. Characters who have come, presumably, from Downstairs appear from Right of window. Left of window is a low bookcase, on the top of which is a handsome vase flanked by candlesticks. Also, the phone.*

TIME: *Late afternoon in November. It is dark outside and the LAMPS are lit as well as WALL-BRACKETS, Down Left and Right.*

AT RISE: *The Stage is empty. Immediately, however, we hear a KEY in the lock of the front door, and* DIANE *comes in, carrying a bag of groceries. She is a blonde, pretty, but a bit on the buxom side. As she enters, another girl,* OLIVE, *comes from door Left. She is*

5

dark, smart-looking. She has a piece of paper in her hand.

OLIVE. If you got that stuff at the A. and P. or the First National, you can take it right back. (*The* OTHER *stares at her.*) Unless it's things we can keep in the freezer for tomorrow.

DIANE. What are you talking about? (*She manages to get the bundle onto a chair.*)

OLIVE. We're dining out.

DIANE. (*Disappointed.*) Not me. I'm tired. I'm getting into pajamas and eating at home. And as for taking anything back to a supermarket—ha! This time of day it's hard enough to get anything out of there, much less putting it back in. Oh! My feet! A woman ran over me with a shopping cart! A little boy stuck me with a pin, and coming out I tripped over a police dog. He was tied with his leash right across the doorway. And I had to fight him for my pork chops. (*She sinks, wearily, onto the sofa.*)

OLIVE. Don't get comfortable. I tell you we've got to go out for dinner.

DIANE. Why?

OLIVE. (*Waving the paper at her.*) On account of this. From Maudie. Listen! I found it on the table there. (*She reads.*) "Dear Olive and Diane. You two must be out of here by seven o'clock, and you can't come back until eleven-thirty. This is Thursday night, and I am exercising my constitutional right."

DIANE. What does she mean? "Constitutional right"?

OLIVE. Oh, you know. The bargain we made. One night each week. The apartment was to be left to one of us, and the other two had to get out and leave the coast clear.

DIANE. Oh, that.

OLIVE. Yes. That! Tuesday night is your night—mine's Wednesday—and Maudie's is Thursday.

DIANE. Yes, yes, but Maudie—Maudie's never exercised her what-you-may-call-it. Her—ha! "Constitutional right."

OLIVE. I know. That's because poor little Maudie never had a boy friend before.

DIANE. (*Gets to her feet.*) You mean she's entertaining a *man? Maudie?*

OLIVE. Must be a man.

DIANE. I don't believe it! Where is she?

OLIVE. Out shopping I guess.

DIANE. Maudie doesn't know any men.

OLIVE. She must know this one. And he must be very special. She's going all out. I found a list of the things she's getting. On the kitchen table. Must have made it out—then forgot it.

DIANE. It could be a friend—Betty Wade—or that Jenkins girl—or--or—somebody from the Research Bureau.

OLIVE. I don't think so. Not from that list. Artichokes —avocados—mushroom—blue cheese—asparagus—and— (*She pauses dramatically.*) steak!

DIANE. *Steak?*

OLIVE. Steak. So it must be a man. Nobody in her right mind would buy a steak for another woman to chew up!

DIANE. Who is he? Do you know? (OLIVE *shakes her head.*) Where'd she meet him?

OLIVE. I don't know that. I don't know anything.

DIANE. Where *could* she meet him? You don't think she picked him up at a bar, do you?

OLIVE. Maudie doesn't go to bars. Unless—

DIANE. Unless—?

OLIVE. No, no! I'm sure she wouldn't do that. She doesn't drink.

DIANE. I wish you'd finish that "unless."

OLIVE. I started to say--er—well, you know how it is these days. Girls get a little desperate sometimes. You know, for the society of that rare bird, known as "the male"!

DIANE. Yeah. I know what you mean. Dinner—with a lot of other women! A theatre party— (*Through her teeth.*) "Oh, such fun! Six of us! All women!" "I'm off to the Catskills for my vacation!" Just us girls, you know. Isn't it lovely?" Ugh! "Maybe we'll run into the ghost of old Henry Hudson and his bowling team!" So if a girl did go to a bar—even to swap "hello's" with the bartender—

OLIVE. No. Maudie wouldn't do that. I'm sure she wouldn't.

DIANE. Then where *did* she meet him?

OLIVE. Well, you and I don't do too badly.

DIANE. No. But you work in an office—a big office. Besides the office force you see customers—or clients— or what-have-you. You go to lunch with a gang—one thing leads to another—

OLIVE. You mean, one man leads to another.

DIANE. Yes. Me, I'm in a bank. The place is crawling with males. Most of 'em I admit, are baldish and plumpish—and they have wives tucked away in White Plains—or Scarsdale—or—Tuckahoe—

OLIVE. Sounds like a song. (*Sings to "Avalon."*) "My wife's tucked away in Tuckahoe"!

DIANE. But occasionally—just occasionally—I meet one who's escaped the hunters. But Maudie! She's with a Research Bureau! She looks up things—in *libraries*. Now I ask you, what sort of man would you meet in a public library?

OLIVE. Oh, she goes other places sometimes. Places like —well, the Museum of Natural History.

DIANE. Ha! What a break! And what sort of man would you meet in the Museum of Natural History, for goodness sake? Neanderthal? I went there once—and except for some school kids—there was nobody in there under a hundred and two. (*The front door is opened, and* MAUDIE *comes in. She is laden down with two enormous shopping bags, filled to overflowing.* MAUDIE *is in the twenties—about the same age as the other two, but rather small, slim. Her coloring is a bit nondescript.*) You lugged all that from the A and P?

MAUDIE: From Gristede's—and the Gourmet Shop—and the Bois de Boulogne Pastry. I took a taxi. (*She has put down her two bundles on a chair; now she hurries to front door.*) The taxi-driver's bringing up the rest of the things. (*She disappears out of sight, to speak to someone just Off Right.*) Thank you. And thanks for waiting and everything. Here's five dollars. Keep the change.

DIANE. "Hello, folks. I'm Amy Vanderbilt." (MAUDIE *reappears, carrying two more bundles.*) What are you giving tonight? One of those "hundred-dollars-a-plate dinners" for the poor starving politicians?

MAUDIE. (*Smiles sweetly.*) I don't want to hurry you girls, but—well, if you're going to change your clothes or anything before you go out—

OLIVE. Look, Maudie—about this man who's coming tonight. It—er—*is* a man, isn't it?

MAUDIE. He was at lunch time.

OLIVE. You had lunch with him?

MAUDIE. That new Swedish place. Royal Smorsgabord. I never could say it right. All you can eat for six dollars a head.

DIANE. Six *dollars?* He must have money.

MAUDIE. I wouldn't know. (*She has begun to take a few things out of the packages: a box of salted almonds, cheese tid-bits.*)

OLIVE. You've had lunch with him before?

MAUDIE. Oh, yes. Several times. That's why I thought I'd like to have him up here. You know, a simple little dinner at home.

DIANE. Simple? You must have spent a week's salary.

MAUDIE. Oh, well. When it's somebody special. Besides, he's bringing the wine and the flowers and the candy—

DIANE. How do you know?

MAUDIE. I don't *know*—but he's the type.

OLIVE. Hm. Along with the wine—he—er—might bring cocktails, too, huh?

MAUDIE. He might.

OLIVE. Or even a bottle of whiskey. (*Very seriously.*) Sit down, Maudie.

MAUDIE. "Sit down"? With all I've got to do, you're asking me to—?

OLIVE. Yes. Please! This is important!

MAUDIE. Oh, well. But make it snappy!

OLIVE. This man—who's coming tonight—who is he?

MAUDIE. Oh, just a—a man I know.

DIANE. Where'd you meet him?

MAUDIE. (*With a shrug.*) Oh—around about.

DIANE. What do you mean? "Around about"? Around about what?

MAUDIE. Around about the end of October.

DIANE. No, no! Around about where?

MAUDIE. Around about Madison Avenue and Thirty-ninth street.

DIANE. You picked him up off the *street?*

MAUDIE. No. I fell down and he picked me up.

DIANE. I don't believe you. (MAUDIE *just grins.*) I see. You don't intend to tell us anything about him.

MAUDIE. I don't know why I should, do you?

OLIVE. Yes, because you—look, Maudie. This is hard to say but—you—you don't know about men—

MAUDIE. About time I learned, don't you think? I'm certainly not going to spend the next forty years in the Public Library.

OLIVE. What I mean, dear—this man who's coming tonight. You here alone with him. Suppose he got fresh—or frisky—or playful—or something? You wouldn't know what to do.

MAUDIE. I'd send him home.

OLIVE. There! You see? You can't always do that. Sometimes they won't go. Especially if they have a few drinks under their belt.

MAUDIE. Then I'll scream.

DIANE. In New York? Ha! Scream in this town and everybody runs off in the opposite direction.

OLIVE. With us, it's different. Diane there—she's a big, strong, hefty, husky girl who—

DIANE. (*Miffed.*) Well, really, Olive! You make me sound like a Notre Dame football tackle.

OLIVE. You know what I mean. Me, I've had Karate lessons. And I sometimes slip a pair of brass knuckles in my bra. But *you,* Maudie—

MAUDIE. I know. I'm a small, skinny, undersized little shrimp who—

OLIVE. I didn't mean anything like that at all.

MAUDIE. Don't worry. I can defend myself— (*A slight pause.*) if I want to.

DIANE. If you *want* to?

OLIVE. Maudie, you—you haven't done anything—er —wrong, have you?

MAUDIE. (*Smiles sweetly.*) N-n-no. Not yet.

OLIVE. Oh! I think we'll stay and meet this man!

MAUDIE. (*Rising angrily.*) And I think you won't! Now you listen to me! I clear out on Tuesdays for Diane —and on Wednesdays for you! So if you don't clear out for *me,* I'll go inside—pack my bags—and get out of here! And you can match out who pays my share of next month's rent—and the telephone and the—the— Remember, *you* signed the lease. I didn't!

DIANE. Oh, well, if you feel that way—

MAUDIE. I do. (*Looks at watch.*) You've got about ten minutes. A little less.

OLIVE. But couldn't we just stay and meet him— just—?

MAUDIE. No!

DIANE. But we could help you get things ready.

MAUDIE. I've got help, thank you. (*The BUZZER sounds. She crosses and opens front door.*) Oh, come in, Sue.

SUE. Am I late—or early—or—?

MAUDIE. Right on the button. Let me take your coat.

SUE. (*Waving at the other* Two.) Hi, girls!

DIANE and OLIVE. Hello, Sue.

MAUDIE. (*On way to coat closet.*) The girls were just leaving. (*She looks at her wrist watch.*) At least—in about eight and a half minutes. (*She gives them a toothy smile.*)

DIANE. You going to have dinner here?

SUE. Oh, no, I'm just the flunkey. I can only stay a short while. (*To* MAUDIE.) Remember I'm a "plain cook," so don't ask me to stuff snails or flap crepes Suzettes—or—

MAUDIE. Oh, I'll do the cooking. You just help get things ready. First, get these things to the kitchen. That shopping bag. No, not that one. The other one. That one stays here.

(*She picks up the two paper bags, and goes out through archway.* SUE *picks up a shopping bag, and starts to follow.*)

OLIVE. Sue! Wait a minute. (SUE *stops.* OLIVE *goes to her and lowers her voice.*) We're terribly worried about Maudie.

SUE. Oh? Why?

OLIVE. Because in all the time we've lived together, she's never entertained a man here before.

DIANE. So far as I know she's never even had a date.

SUE. Poor Maudie!

OLIVE. Exactly. That's why we— Who is this man? Do you know? (SUE *shakes her head.*) She didn't tell you? (*Again the head-shake.*)

DIANE. But didn't you ask?

SUE. Nope.

DIANE. But that's unnatural. You're a woman. Aren't you curious?

SUE. Of course. About to bust.

DIANE. Then why didn't you—?

SUE. Listen. I was brought up with four brothers—all older than me. Every time I asked one of them, "Where you going?"—"Who were you with?"—"What time did

you get in last night"—I got my ears pinned back. I
never ask questions. I won't even go up to a policeman
and ask him how to get to the B.M.T. subway. (*She
goes out through archway.*)

DIANE. Well, we didn't get much out of her.

OLIVE. Maudie's primed her.

DIANE. Olive! Let's go—wait a little while—then come
back.

OLIVE. No! We can't do that!

DIANE. We could pretend we've forgotten something.
(*But* OLIVE *shakes her head.*) But I want to see this
man! I want to find out who he is! I've *got* to. I can't
bear it! (*A slight pause.*) Anyway—it's for her own
good.

OLIVE. (*Doubtfully.*) Well. We'd have to be awfully
careful. Little Maudie's got a temper. She meant what
she said about packing up. I'm fond of Maudie. And
she's good about housework—and doing the dishes—
and— Besides she might bolt the door—put the chain
on. She wouldn't let us in.

DIANE. (*Suddenly.*) I know. The fire escape. (*She
points to it.*) We never think of locking that window.

OLIVE. But how'll we get on it?

DIANE. Easy. The superintendent. We'll tell him
Maudie's gone to sleep with the door bolted. He'd do it.

OLIVE. Sort of a dirty trick, don't you think?

DIANE. Of course it is. But, well, you have to fight fire
with fire. Whatever that means. (MAUDIE *returns through
archway. She looks at the other* TWO, *then looks pointedly
at her wrist watch.*) Oh, we're going! We're going! Aren't
we, Olive? (*Elaborately.*) We thought we'd go over to
Lorenzo's for spaghetti, take in a movie—and we won't
be back until eleven-thirty.

MAUDIE. (*Sweetly.*) Thank you. You're so good to me.
(*She gets busy setting up the gate-leg table.*)

DIANE. Just one thing. You asked Sue Baxter to help
you get things ready. She might still be here when the—
er—your guest arrives.

MAUDIE. She might.

DIANE. Then she might meet him.

MAUDIE. She might. Yes.

DIANE. Well, why couldn't you have asked one of *us* to help you get things ready?

MAUDIE. Then *you'd* meet him, huh?

DIANE. Yes.

MAUDIE. Oh, no! Not on your life!

DIANE. But why? What's the difference between having Sue and one of us? Both of us, for that matter?

MAUDIE. (*Busy with table.*) All the difference in the world. Sue's got her man.

OLIVE. What?

MAUDIE. A navy lieutenant. She's engaged. Wild about him. Wouldn't look at another man.

DIANE. Oh—you think we would, eh?

OLIVE. You mean you think one of us might try to take your—this man away from you?

MAUDIE. I wouldn't put it past you.

DIANE. (*Offended.*) Oh! I think you're being insulting.

MAUDIE. Nope. Just cautious. Competition being what it is today.

OLIVE. Honestly, Maudie, do you seriously think that one of us—?

MAUDIE. I notice you never let Diane meet *your* dates —and vice versa—

OLIVE. But we're your friends—your roommates— your—

MAUDIE. (*That sweet smile again.*) I've seen two little fuzzy kittens tear each other to pieces over a tiny bite of tuna fish.

DIANE. This is too much. I'm getting out of here. Come on, Ol! (*She starts for front door.* OLIVE *starts to follow.*)

OLIVE. Yes. I guess we'd better. But I think you ought to know, Maudie, you've hurt me very much. (*She goes out.*)

DIANE. Me, too. And I hope the man, when he gets

here, turns out to be a gorilla—and that he chokes you to
death.

*(She goes out, slamming door. MAUDIE smiles. At that
second, SUE returns from kitchen with some table
silver, etc. During the next few speeches, MAUDIE
gets a table cover out of drawer of lowboy and the
TWO set the table.)*

SUE. Finally get rid of 'em?

MAUDIE. Yes. But I've got a sneaking idea, they're
going to try and come back.

SUE. Why?

MAUDIE. Diane, because she has to *know* everything.
She's a natural-born snooper. She reads people's post
cards—holds letters up to the light—rattles packages. She
can't help it, I guess. I think all her ancestors were
maiden ladies. You know. A village street—lace curtains
—and a pair of binoculars.

SUE. *(Laughs.)* And Olive? *(They are still busy with
the table-setting.)*

MAUDIE. The same. With a difference. Olive "protects"
me! She thinks I'm four years old—and a double-bar-
relled nit-wit to boot. When I go out, she's at the door
with an umbrella, galoshes, and a spray gun. She means
well, but— Oh!

SUE. That's why you don't want them to meet this
man, huh?

MAUDIE. I'd die! Simply die!

SUE. Maudie! I've never seen you so determined.

MAUDIE. I have reason to be.

SUE. You could put on the bolt—use the chain.

MAUDIE. No. Olive would call a cop—have the door
smashed in.

SUE. Why?

MAUDIE. To save me from a "fate worse than death
itself."

SUE. You're kidding. Then what are you going to—?

MAUDIE. Circumstantial evidence!

SUE. What *are* you talking about?

MAUDIE. They wouldn't *dare* actually come out to the kitchen. I threatened to move out if they tried any funny stuff. The man'll be out there, helping me cook dinner. (*She suddenly goes to telephone and starts dialing.*) Sue. Go to that other shopping bag and get out that bottle of wine. The other things too.

SUE. (*She does so.*) Wine. Oh! Flowers! They're all crushed. Why did you put beautiful roses like this in a shopping bag?

MAUDIE. I couldn't bring 'em in a box. The girls would have seen it. Stick 'em in that vase there. I'll put some water in later.

SUE. Candy, too? Seems to me the *man* might contribute a *little* something to the evening's festivities.

MAUDIE. There isn't any man.

(*A long pause.*)

SUE. W-what did you say?

MAUDIE. (*She goes to phone and dials.*) I was going to tell you anyway. There isn't any man.

SUE. There isn't any—?

MAUDIE. Sh-h! (*Into phone.*) Mrs. Edwards? . . . Oh. She isn't? . . . Oh. Well, may I speak to *Mr.* Edwards then? . . . Oh! Then—excuse me for asking, but who is this? . . . Oh, I see. The baby-sitter. Well, listen— Oh, I know you, don't I? Judy, isn't it? . . . Oh. Sorry. June. Yes. I'm Maud Hollins from downstairs. I met you once when . . . Yes. Yes, that's it! . . . Oh, fine, thanks. Look. I'd like to ask a favor . . . I'm sure Mr. Edwards wouldn't mind. I—I want to borrow a coat . . . No, no! A *man's* coat. A coat of Mr. Edwards' . . . Yes . . . Oh, any kind. Top coat— overcoat—raincoat—it doesn't matter . . . Yes. And a hat. If he has another hat he isn't wearing tonight . . . Yes . . . What? . . . Well, you see I—well, it's sort

of a joke. I want to dress up—for a gag, you know . . .
Yes. I'll return them later in the evening . . . Yes . . .
Oh, you will? Oh, thanks. Thanks ever so much. (*She
hangs up.*) Nice kid. She'll bring them down to me.

SUE. Just a minute! Will you please be good enough
to tell me what all this is about?

MAUDIE. Yes. But let's get this table set. Get those
candlesticks. Those silver bowls. Dress up the place. Oh,
and an ashtray.

SUE. Listen. I'm not doing another thing until you tell
me. You say there—there *isn't* any man?

MAUDIE. That's right.

SUE. Wait a minute! Let me get this! There isn't any
man coming, but you're going to pretend there is. Is that
right?

MAUDIE. Yes. I'm going to fix things up—cook the
food—and serve it. Then, later, I'm going to mess up the
table—throw part of the food down the incinerator—
pour out the wine—crumple up the napkins—make it look
just like two people had been dining. Look. I've even
got a cigar butt. (*She opens her purse and takes out a
Kleenex. Unwrapping it she discloses a half-smoked cigar.
Gingerly she puts it in the ashtray.*) I got this from the
taxi-driver. I bought it and had him smoke it while I was
in the Gourmet Shop.

SUE. But you could have used a cigarette.

MAUDIE. No. Women smoke cigarettes—but a cigar
spells "man"! M-A-L-E—"MAN"!

SUE. But all this money—all these preparations—
Why are you doing all this?

MAUDIE. Because I'm tired of being "Poor little
Maudie"! That's why!

SUE. What?

MAUDIE. "Poor little Maudie never has a boy-friend."
"Never has a date." "Never has a man for dinner." Twice
a week I scuttle out of here so Diane or Olive can enter-
tain Fred—or—Walter—or Mr. Gawhoozit or somebody
—for dinner. She puts on a dinky, frilly little apron—

sticks a buttercup in her hair—and goes all domestic and homey and cosyfied—so they can see what she'd be like in a vine-covered cottage. So far they haven't snared anybody. But the next morning at breakfast I have to hear what Joe or Fred or Alex or somebody said about politics —or baseball—or the stock market. *I'm sick of it!* You know I don't have any Fred or Alex or Theodore or anybody. *So*—I made one up.

SUE. But surely you—you don't have to go through all this to—to—? You could just say you—you were going out on a date.

MAUDIE. Ha! And you think they'd believe me?

SUE. Wouldn't they?

MAUDIE. Not those two hyenas. They're too smart. And they know me too well. They'd say, "Oh, yeah." And after I'd left they'd say "Poor little Maudie." Oh, I've heard them, when they didn't know I was listening. "Poor little Maudie. We really ought to do something about her."

SUE. Well, why *don't* they do something about you, then?

MAUDIE. Oh, come, Sue! These days a girl's doing well to have *one* man on the string. Who ever heard of a girl with a spare?

SUE. I guess you're right. There must be a hundred thousand bachelors in this town. Where are they? Where do they get to?

MAUDIE. Might as well ask where flies go in the wintertime. (*The BUZZER sounds.* MAUDIE *hurries to front door.*) Oh, come in, June.

(JUNE *enters. She is a girl of about fifteen. She giggles a lot.*)

JUNE. These do?

MAUDIE. Oh, fine. Yes. Thanks ever so much. Miss Baxter, this is June. She baby-sits for the Edwards. When they come back, tell them I'll return these later.

JUNE. Oh, she'll be back real soon. Got to dress to go to the theatre. He's gone to a fight—Madison Square Garden. You say you're gonna dress up—play a joke on somebody?

MAUDIE. Well, sort of. Yes.

JUNE. They'll be too big for you.

MAUDIE. That won't matter. It's just a gag.

JUNE. Oh, well, have fun! (*She goes out front door.*)

SUE. What are they for?

MAUDIE. More circumstantial evidence. Just in case Olive or Diane comes back. (*She pulls out chair Down Right, puts the coat across the back, and the hat on top. She starts Left, looking at table.*) We need wine glasses, water tumblers, more spoons and—I'm going to start the food.

(*She goes out archway Left. SUE follows. There is a slight pause, then a noise at window. The window is carefully opened, and DIANE sticks her head in. Then she quietly slips her leg over the sill and comes cautiously into the room.*)

DIANE. (*In a whisper.*) Come on.

OLIVE. (*Sticks her head in, but doesn't enter.*) It's too early, I tell you. He's not here yet.

DIANE. Say! That's our best table cover!

OLIVE. So what?

DIANE. (*Excitedly moves towards Right.*) He is here, Olive! His coat and hat! (*She puts hat on seat of chair, and holds up coat, to inspect the lining.*) Brooks Brothers. Nothing cheap about this guy. Oh!

OLIVE. What's the matter?

DIANE. (*Disappointed.*) You'd think he'd put his name in the lining somewhere, wouldn't you?

OLIVE. Why should he?

DIANE. Oh, when he hangs it up somewhere he'd be sure to get the right one back.

OLIVE. I guess he knows his own coat.

DIANE. (*Has put down coat and picks up the hat.*) Honestly. His hat hasn't even got his initials in it. I think that's disgusting. Most men have their initials stamped in the lining somewhere. A Dobbs, too. He must be very careless.

OLIVE. Or, maybe, just rich. Come on. It's cold out here.

DIANE. It could be he's just cagey.

OLIVE. I doubt that. He wouldn't know you'd be snooping around.

DIANE. I resent that! I'm not snooping, I just want to— This candy. It's the very best. And these roses. You know what they cost? About ten dollars a dozen!

OLIVE. How do you know?

DIANE. I was going to take some to my uncle in the hospital. I settled for half a dozen daisies.

OLIVE. All right—all right. You've found out all you can about him now, so—

DIANE. Couldn't I just sneak along to the kitchen and—

OLIVE. No! Absolutely not!

DIANE. But I want to *see* him. I want to—

OLIVE. I know you do. And so do I! The only thing is to go back down to the super's apartment—keep warm —and later, when they're having dinner, we can peek in through the window here. (*There is a slight noise Off Left.*) Oh! Someone's coming. Hurry. And be careful!

(*She ducks out of sight.* DIANE *hurries Upstage. As she reaches the window she trips, and falls, knocking over a potted plant which was on the sill.* SUE *has appeared in archway Left.*)

SUE. Well, hello! (DIANE *picks herself up. She is considerably confused.*)

DIANE. Oh. I—I was just closing the window. (*She does so.*)

SUE. (*Not a bit fooled.*) Yeah? Who opened it?

DIANE. I don't know. I really don't know. I certainly didn't. I wouldn't open the window on a night like this. I came back to get my bag. See. (*She reaches down to pick up the bag she just dropped.*)

SUE. You usually keep it on the floor like that?

DIANE. Of course not. But I got all the way over to Lorenzo's and found I didn't have it. (*Tries a laugh.*) Been funny if I got ready to pay the check and didn't have any money, wouldn't it?

SUE. Hilarious. Yes.

DIANE. Well, I'd better get going. Olive's waiting for me. We're having spaghetti over at Anselmo's.

SUE. Lorenzo's.

DIANE. Yes. That's what I meant. So— (*She goes to door, then turns.*) I suppose Maudie and her friend are out cooking dinner.

SUE. That's right.

DIANE. (*Lingering.*) Is he nice?

SUE. Charming.

DIANE. The wine there—it's imported.

SUE. Oh, yes. Imported wine—imported vodka—pinch-bottle Scotch— (*She has moved towards Right.*)

DIANE. He brought all that? I don't know what Olive will say.

SUE. Olive the house-mother?

DIANE. No, but— Well, I really ought to—

SUE. Go. Yes, I wouldn't keep you for the world. (*She all but pushes* DIANE *out the door, closing it after her.*)

DIANE. (*Heard outside, her voice raised in anger.*) You can't put me out of my own house!

(SUE *smiles to herself, then goes to the telephone, and dials.* MAUDIE *returns with glasses, which she puts on the table.*)

SUE. Seeing if I can get Jerry. She did sneak back. Diane. Through the window.

MAUDIE. Oh, no. She didn't!

Sue. (*Nods.*) Don't worry. I gave her a song and dance about— (*Into phone.*) Hello. Can you tell me please if Lieutenant Banning has checked in yet? He has a reservation there . . . Yes, I'll wait. (*To* Maudie.) I told her you and the man were carousing out in the kitchen. Scotch—vodka—

Maudie. Sue! You didn't!

Sue. Why not? Give her something to *really* think about.

Maudie. But Olive! If Olive finds out—

Sue. You're not really carousing. And you've got to get over this thing you've got about Olive. She's not your boss—or— (*Into phone.*) Oh, thank you. I'd like to leave a message . . . When he comes in—

Maudie. Have him call you here. (*She goes out Left.*)

Sue. When he comes in, have him ring Regent 4-8715. Yes . . . That's it. As soon as he gets there . . . Thank you. (*She hangs up. As she does so, the BUZZER sounds.* Sue *goes to open front door.* June *comes in quickly, carrying some clothes.*) Hello.

June. Can't stop, but I thought if Miss Hollins is gonna dress up, she'd want these too.

Sue. What are they?

June. (*As she throws them, one by one, on sofa.*) A shirt and a tie—a sports jacket—and a pair of slacks.

Sue. Oh, but she won't need all those things. It was just—

June. It's all right. Mr. Edwards won't mind. I gotta go. The baby's squawking. (*She darts out.*)

Sue. Well, thanks, thanks.

(*But the door is closed.* Sue *gives the table a once-over, picks up a salted almond which she puts into her mouth and goes out Left. There is a very slight pause, then the window is quietly opened, and* Olive *is seen.*)

Olive. (*In a whisper.*) Diane! Diane! (*She slips*

quietly into the room, and looks about. She moves Down-
stage, and a bit towards archway Left. She listens for
any sounds Off Left. Now DIANE *appears on the fire*
escape. Climbing in, she knocks over another flower pot.
OLIVE *hurries towards her.*) For goodness' sake! What
became of you?

DIANE. I had to go out through the door. That Sue
came snooping around.

OLIVE. And caught you?

DIANE. Yes. I hate sneaky people. (*She moves around
Left end of sofa, to in front of it.*)

OLIVE. Well, for goodness sake; let's get out. I only
came back to look for you. (*At Right of table, she suddenly points.*) Oh, what are those things? Over the arm
of the sofa?

DIANE. (*She goes to investigate.*) Clothes.

OLIVE. Clothes?

DIANE. (*Enumerates, as she holds them up.*) A shirt—
a tie—a sports jacket and a—a—a pair of pants!

OLIVE. Oh, no! NO!

DIANE. But—but what does it mean?

OLIVE. Well, if you don't know—

DIANE. No! Oh, Olive! You don't think— But I
thought he was out in the kitchen—cooking dinner.

OLIVE. That kitchen doesn't get so hot, you have to
stand over the oven in your underwear! (*She starts for
Left.*)

DIANE. Where are you going?

OLIVE. I'm going to break his neck.

DIANE. Wait!

OLIVE. Maybe not his neck, but an arm—and a couple
of ribs. (*She stops to take a stance for Karate.*) I'm out
of practice but— Put your left foot forward—your right
arm extended—bring your left down and under—

DIANE. No! Wait! (*She has been examining the sports
jacket.*)

OLIVE. What's the use of that? If his name wasn't in
his top coat, it won't be in—

DIANE. (*Has examined inside pocket of jacket.*) But it is! It is! Oh, no! NO! Oh, Olive! *OLIVE!*

OLIVE. What's the matter? Someone we know? (*She moves towards Right.*)

DIANE. (*Reads.*) "Hugh D. Edwards"!

OLIVE. Hugh D.— From *upstairs?* I don't believe it!

DIANE. Look, then! Look! (OLIVE *does look. The two* GIRLS *stare at each other.*) What are we going to do?

OLIVE. (*Reverts to a whisper.*) I don't know. (*Then suddenly.*) Yes, I do too! (*She stalks to the telephone.*)

DIANE. What are you going to do? Call the police?

OLIVE. I'm going to do better than that! I'm going to call Mrs. Edwards. (*She picks up the phone.*) What's the number?

DIANE. W-what?

OLIVE. (*Impatiently.*) The number! The number! You're always chatting with her! What's the—

DIANE. Oh. It's Regent 4-2866—no! 8266—or is it 86—

OLIVE. Oh, for goodness' sake. Never mind! I'll go get her! (*She strides towards door Right.*)

DIANE. Well, I do know it. But I'm so upset I—I—

OLIVE. (*Flings open the front door.*) Oh! Mrs. Edwards! Is that you?

MRS. EDWARDS. (*Her voice heard outside.*) Why, yes. Hello, Olive! Just got in. I have to change to—

OLIVE. Will you come in here, please, Mrs. Edwards. It's very important!

(*Leaving the door open, she hastily gathers up jacket, slacks, etc., and puts them behind her. She is facing door as* MRS. EDWARDS *comes in. She is a sweet-faced little woman in the early forties.*)

MRS. EDWARDS. (*To* DIANE.) Oh, hello, I've only got a moment. I— Oh! Is something wrong?

OLIVE. Very much wrong, I'm afraid.

MRS. EDWARDS. Oh! A burglary! We've had another burglary?

OLIVE. No. It isn't that. It's— Mrs. Edwards, where is your husband?

MRS. EDWARDS. (*In alarm.*) Oh! Something's happened to him! What is it? Tell me!

OLIVE. No, no, it isn't—nothing's happened to him. Yet!

MRS. EDWARDS. Yet? What do you mean?

OLIVE. Where did your husband tell you he was going tonight?

MRS. EDWARDS. To the fight. Madison Square Garden. Why? You mean he didn't go? (OLIVE *shakes her head.*) Where is he then?

DIANE. He's out in our kitchen—in his B.V.D.'s.

OLIVE. (*To* DIANE.) Men don't wear B.V.D.'s any more.

DIANE. I wouldn't know about that. And how would *you* know?

OLIVE. Please! Whatever he's wearing—or *not* wearing —the fact remains he's out there and what the newspapers would call "improperly clad."

MRS. EDWARDS. W-what? What on earth is he doing out there?

DIANE. Sizzling steaks! At least we *hope* they're sizzling steaks!

MRS. EDWARDS. I don't believe it!

OLIVE. You don't? Look at these then. (*Showing her the clothes.*) Is this your husband's? And this—and this —and *these?*

MRS. EDWARDS. Yes. Yes. Yes. But how—I mean what —you said "they," who's they?

OLIVE. Poor little Maudie.

MRS. EDWARDS. Little Maudie? You mean Maude— your roommate? Oh, no! He—he wouldn't!

OLIVE. (*Points.*) See? A table set for two. He brought flowers—candy—wine.

DIANE. (*Excitedly.*) And vodka—and pinch-bottle Scotch! (*To* OLIVE.) You didn't know that, did you?

OLIVE. He's worse than I thought!

MRS. EDWARDS. I still don't believe it!

OLIVE. Would you like to go see for yourself?

MRS. EDWARDS. I certainly would! (*She starts for Left.*)

DIANE. (*Hurrying.*) I'll go with you!

MRS. EDWARDS. No, thank you!

DIANE. But I can show you the way and where—

MRS. EDWARDS. (*Effectively blocking* DIANE.) No! That won't be necessary. My apartment upstairs has the same arrangement as this one. Remember? This is *my* affair—and I prefer to handle it privately. (*With dignity, she goes out through archway.*)

DIANE. Well—snooty, isn't she? (*Listens at archway.*) Maybe she won't close the connecting door—and we can hear what—

OLIVE. No! Get away from there! Stop snooping!

DIANE. "Snooping"? Well, I like that!

OLIVE. Things are bad enough! You keep out of it! We've done our duty and— Poor little Maudie!

DIANE. An old man like that! Why, he must be forty if he's a day!

OLIVE. The older they are, the worse they get. Or hadn't you noticed?

DIANE. Of course I've noticed. Why, I remember one time— Never mind. (*She sits in chair Right of table. Takes some salted almonds.*)

OLIVE. You can eat at a time like this!

DIANE. (*A bit venomously.*) Well, I'm a "hefty, husky girl," remember? And you've made me miss my dinner.

OLIVE. (*Indignantly.*) Just a moment! It was *I* who made you miss your— Whose idea was it to climb up the fire escape?

DIANE. Well, you came behind me!

OLIVE. Oh, please! (*A slight pause.*)

DIANE. I wonder who'll get the children.

OLIVE. What children?

DIANE. The Edwards' children. After the divorce.

OLIVE. Oh, she will. No judge would give them to a man like that!

DIANE. Will we have to testify? In court, I mean?

OLIVE. Depends on where she gets the divorce. If she gets it in the State of New York, we would.

DIANE. (*Rather likes the idea.*) I've never been in court. They take pictures, don't they! Hmmmm. Do we wear hats?

OLIVE. (*Her mind on other things.*) What are you talking about?

DIANE. About court. Is it like church—where you have to have your head covered, or can you—?

OLIVE. (*Snaps at her.*) How would I know? Turn on Perry Mason.

DIANE. Maybe she won't get a divorce. Sometimes these days—the world being so unsettled and everything—a woman who's got a firm grip on a man is liable to hang on—no matter what he does. She can't be sure of getting another one. (MRS. EDWARDS *comes in from archway Left. On her face there is a rather curious expression— an expression that is often referred to as that of the cat who ate the canary. She wears a slight smile, her eyes are dancing, and her manner ever so slightly smug. Both* GIRLS *rise;* DIANE *goes towards her.*) Well? What did he say?

MRS. EDWARDS. He—didn't say much of anything. Just —er—"How do you do?"

OLIVE. "How do you DO?" Caught red-handed and all he says is "How do you do?"

DIANE. But didn't you question him? (*The* OTHER *shakes her head.*) But—but don't you *care?* Or has it happened before?

MRS. EDWARDS. No, it's never happened before.

DIANE. Then why didn't you question him?

MRS. EDWARDS. I didn't think I had a right to.

OLIVE. Oh, come, Mrs. Edwards, please! I'm as broad-minded as the next one, but well, fun's fun, but— Oh! (*Words fail her.*)

MRS. EDWARDS. I didn't question him, you see, because he's not my husband.

OLIVE. Not your—the man out there is not your husband.

DIANE. Are you sure?

MRS. EDWARDS. Well, really.

DIANE. I mean—

OLIVE. But if he's not your husband, why was he wearing your husband's clothes?

MRS. EDWARDS. I don't think he *was* wearing my husband's clothes.

DIANE. Then what clothes *was* he wearing?

MRS. EDWARDS. His own, I imagine. The ones he has on now.

DIANE. You mean he's—he's—

MRS. EDWARDS. Oh, yes. He's wearing everything the well-dressed man *should* wear—even to a boutonniere.

DIANE. Oh!

OLIVE. Look, Mrs. Edwards. If the man out there isn't your—your—how do you explain *those things!*

MRS. EDWARDS. I don't attempt to. But I'm sure there's some simple explanation. When I get back from the theatre—and my husband returns from the prize fight, I'll ask him.

DIANE. Not till then? We can't wait! We want to know *now!*

MRS. EDWARDS. I'm afraid you'll have to wait, because I certainly don't intend to have my husband paged at Madison Square Garden. Well—I must go change. (*She picks up gloves she had left on gate-leg table.*)

OLIVE. Just a moment, Mrs. Edwards. Please. That man out there— Who is he?

MRS. EDWARDS. I haven't the dimmest idea.

DIANE. But didn't you ask him?

MRS. EDWARDS. Certainly not.

DIANE. And you don't even know who he *is?*

MRS. EDWARDS. Little Maudie introduced us, of course, but I didn't quite catch his name.

DIANE. But surely—you know what he looks like.

MRS. EDWARDS. Oh, yes. I was sure you'd ask, so I noticed particularly. He's about six foot one-and-a-half, I'd say. Broad shoulders—slim at the waist. He has blue eyes, but his hair is coal black. A fascinating combination, I always think. He has a strong, rather aquiline face, but very handsome in a virile, masculine way. And—let's see now! Oh, yes. And from the little time that I was with him, I found him utterly, *utterly* charming! That's about all, I believe. (*She goes to front door, and turns back.*) Oh! Since I know how interested you are—both of you— and since of course you won't be seeing him yourselves, if there's anything else I can think of about him, I'll telephone you tomorrow. (*With a smile of the cat who's eaten not only a canary, but a sixteen-pound turkey, she goes out.*)

OLIVE. That had all the earmarks of a very nasty crack in the rib-section.

DIANE. (*A bit stunned.*) W-what?

OLIVE. All that about—"Since you won't be seeing him yourselves"! Ha! Maudie must have told her about our little arrangement.

DIANE. (*Unhappily.*) No. I did. One day when—oh, never mind. "Charming." Hm. Just what Sue said. (*A slight pause.*) I can't stand this! (*She heads for archway Left.*)

OLIVE. No, you don't! We have a code. Remember? A code of honor!

DIANE. A code of honor among women? I never heard of such a thing! (*Again she turns.*)

OLIVE. All right! But if you go out there, not only will little Maudie pack up and move out, but I will too. And I'd like to remind you. When we signed the lease, your name came first.

(SUE *comes through the archway with a pitcher of water.*)

SUE. (*To* DIANE, *in pretended surprise.*) Welll! You

back again? What did you leave this time? (DIANE *glares at her.*) Olive, too. I wonder who keeps opening this window. B'rrr! (*She puts pitcher on table and goes to close it.*) Oh! You broke another flower pot, didn't you? You know, if you're going to keep this up, you ought to write to the Library of Congress. Get one of those little pamphlets they put out. They have them for almost everything. I'm sure there's one—"How to Be a Cat Burglar"! (*She starts picking up broken flower pots.*)

DIANE. (*Gives her another dirty look, then turns towards Right.*) Come on, Ol!

SUE. Oh, off to Lorenzo's—Anselmo's—Antonio's—or—?

DIANE. Yes, we're off! But I must say I don't feel much like spaghetti at the moment! What's that odor coming from the kitchen? What are they cooking out there?

SUE. Oh, Porterhouse steak with mushrooms, asparagus with Hollandaise, potatoes au gratin,—

DIANE. Ugh! (*She hurries out Right.* SUE *smiles.*)

OLIVE. I want you to know, Sue, that whatever spying I do on little Maudie, it's for her own good.

SUE. Oh, yeah?

OLIVE. I'm very fond of Maudie. I'd do anything for her.

SUE. Then may I suggest that you do something for her that will *really* help? Leave her alone!

OLIVE. But she's so sort of—inexperienced—naïve—undeveloped—

SUE. I wouldn't say that. She's developed quite a bit in the last ten minutes. (*She returns to table.*)

OLIVE. Oh. You mean on account of the—the man out there?

SUE. Yes. She seems sure of herself—her eyes are sparkling. I persuaded her to slip in, put on the new dinner dress she's never worn—fix her hair differently. Oh, too bad you can't see her. But I know you have to hurry off with Diane.

OLIVE. Yes. (*She turns towards door.*) Just one thing. Those clothes there— (*She points to sofa.*)

SUE. (*Picks up pitcher of water; during these next few speeches, she fills tumbler, and vase of flowers.*) Oh, those. They're mine.

OLIVE. *Yours?* With "Hugh D. Edwards" in the coat?

SUE. Yes. You see Jerry—that's my fiancé—got an unexpected leave. Navy. Flew in from Pensacola. But he couldn't get a through plane. They put him down in Atlanta—Baltimore—Philadelphia. When he got to the hotel he was pretty well mussed up. He sent his uniform out to be pressed—and some idiot bellhop—or tailor—or somebody—delivered it to the wrong room. They can't locate the uniform—they can't even locate the idiot. I told Maudie about it—she's seen Jerry—and she thought Mr. Edwards upstairs would be about his size. So—I'm taking them down to him.

OLIVE. Oh. But what about the shirt and tie?

SUE. (*Smiles.*) Oh, that was the baby-sitter's idea. She just threw them in for good measure.

OLIVE. I see. Well, I guess there's nothing more I can do here— (*Rather reluctantly, she opens the front door.*)

SUE. (*Sweetly.*) I guess not. Enjoy your spaghetti!

OLIVE. I *hate* spaghetti!

(*She goes closing the door.* MAUDIE *appears in archway. She has fixed her hair, and she is wearing a becoming dinner gown.*)

SUE. Maudie! You look *lovely!*

MAUDIE. I don't know why I had to get all fixed up this way.

SUE. (*Laughs.*) For the man who didn't come to dinner. Maudie, I've got the strangest feeling. That something wonderful is going to happen.

MAUDIE. It hasn't yet. What makes you think that?

SUE. Because we deserve it! The narrow squeaks we've had—the stories we've made up—the explanations we—

Ha! I wonder what that nice Mrs. Edwards said to those two pussy-footin' female gum-shoes. She said she'd blast their ear-drums. I wonder—

(*The PHONE rings.* SUE *hurries to answer it.*)

MAUDIE. That'll be Jerry.

SUE. (*At phone.*) Hello . . . JERRY, DARLING. Oh, Jerry! . . . What? . . . Of course I do! . . . Yes, I—I— What? . . . Yes. I'll be right down . . . Yes. I'll take a cab—and meet you in the lobby . . . Yes, I . . . What? . . . *What did you say?* . . . Oh! For your friend? What's his name? . . . Oh. Yes. You tell Steve I've got a wonderful gal for him. She's right here now. (*She looks at* MAUDIE.)

MAUDIE. No, no!

SUE. (*Into phone.*) Tell Steve she's lovely—and attractive—and—

MAUDIE. I'm not! I'm not lovely—and I'm not attractive—and I—

SUE. (*Laughs. Into phone.*) She says she's *not* lovely— *not* attractive! But she is really! The only trouble with her is she has two horrible, nasty, mean *step*-sisters! They make her sweep in the chimney corner—while they go dashing off to balls and meet princes and—JERRY! How would you and Steve like a steak dinner? Porterhouse steak—and all the trimmings! . . . You come up here then. And *afterwards* we can do the town . . . Yes. Right away. Hop in a cab and— Oh, the address is 396 East Eighty-second street! Second floor . . . Hurry, darling! I'm dying to see you. (*She hangs up.*)

MAUDIE. Oh, Sue! Sue! Do you—do you think he'll like me?

SUE. Now stop that! Let's get going! We have to set four places instead of— *Oh! The steaks!* Turn 'em off! Men like their steaks rare! So you— No! I'll do that! *You*—get rid of those clothes! Hide them—or something.

MAUDIE. (*Gathering up clothes.*) You now Mrs. Edwards told me once that when she married her husband he was in the Marines.

SUE. Yeah? Then you get those things *out of here!* Way out! Take them upstairs. All we need now is to have the Navy arrive and find the Marines were here ahead of them!

(*She hurries out Left;* MAUDIE *hurries out Right, as:*)

THE CURTAIN FALLS

PROPERTY PLOT

Sofa—R. C.
Coffee Table—before sofa—R. C.
Side Chair—D. R.
Table—U. R.
Bookcase—U. L. C.
Low Boy—U. L.
Armchair—D. L.
Gateleg Table—L. C.
Side Chair—above table
Side Chair—R. of table
Side Chair—L. of table

On Table—U. R. :
  Lamp
  Bonbon Dishes

On Coffee Table:
  Magazines
  Ashtray

At Window:
  Drapes
  Shade
  4 Potted Plants on Window Sill

On Low Boy:
  Lamp
  In Drawer of Low Boy—Table Cover, napkins

On Bookcase:
  2 Candlesticks—with candles
  Flower Vase
  Telephone
Wall Bracket—(Electric)—D. R.
Wall Bracket—(Electric)—D. L.

OFFSTAGE PROPS

Off Right:
  Bag of Groceries—(Diane)
  2 Shopping Bags—Full—(Maudie)
    In One Shopping Bag:
      Box of Salted Nuts
      Box of Cheese Crackers
    In Other Shopping Bag—(Concealed)
      Bottle of Imported Wine
      5 Pound Box of Candy
      Dozen Roses
  2 Paper Bags of Groceries—Full—(Maudie)
  In Maudie's Handbag—Half-smoked Cigar, wrapped in
    Kleenex
  Man's Hat—(June)
  Man's Topcoat—(June)
  Man's Jacket—(June)
  Man's Shirt—(June)
  Tie—(June)

Off Left:
  Sheet of Notepaper—(Olive)
  Silverware (Knives, forks, spoons)—(Sue)
  2 Wine Glasses—(Maudie)
  2 Water Glasses—(Maudie)
  Pitcher of Water—(Sue)

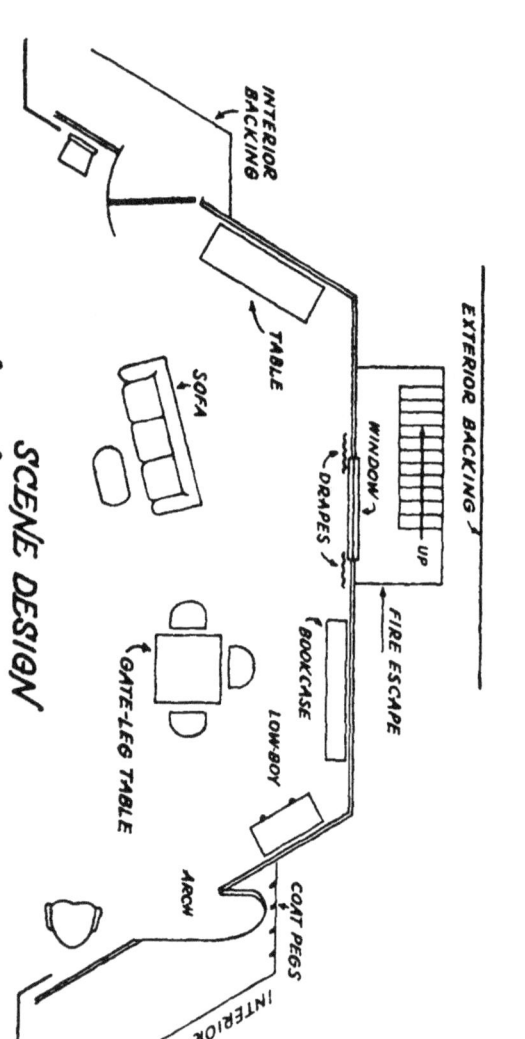

SCENE DESIGN
"WHEN MEN ARE SCARCE"

INTERIOR BACKING

BACKING

EXTERIOR BACKING

TABLE

SOFA

DRAPES

WINDOW

UP

FIRE ESCAPE

BOOKCASE

LOW-BOY

GATE-LEG TABLE

ARCH

COAT PEGS

INTERIOR BACKING